To the Heart of
Difficult Conversations

To the Heart of Difficult Conversations

A collaboration between
Berwick Literary Festival *and* Berwick Academy

Curated and edited by
Chris Adriaanse

Published by
Berwick Literary Festival

Book design by Fogbank Projects
Printed by Martins The Printers, Berwick-upon-Tweed
ISBN 978-1-3999-9523-8

Published by Berwick Literary Festival
berwickliteraryfestival.com

To all the difficult conversations
that were needlessly avoided

This is a Living Heritage project sponsored by:

Create Berwick

It has been funded by:

Table of contents

Why difficult conversations?   9
   Introduction to this project   11
   Introduction from Berwick Literary Festival   12
   Introduction from Berwick Academy   14
A short folktale to begin:
   The Drop of Honey   17
Difficult Conversations by Berwick Academy students   19
   List of contributors   20
   Unspoken words   21
   Rising tensions   31
   Caught in the act   43
   Facing the truth   51
   Clearing the air   61
   Finding support   69
A final folktale to end:
   The Beast of the Bean Garden   79
A mysterious plaque in Tweedmouth   83
About the editor   94
   Acknowledgements   95

Why difficult conversations?

Everyone reading this will have had at least one difficult conversation. You've probably had a lot more. They can be difficult in different ways and at different points. They can start out difficult or become more difficult along the way.

What's fascinating is their variation. No two difficult conversations will be alike and no two people will experience a difficult conversation in the same way.

Maybe it starts as a simple disagreement about what happened – who is right and who is wrong? Who is to blame? Who might be lying? And what this might mean to those involved.

Or maybe tensions arise as emotions begin to surface and feelings of apprehension, fear, anxiety, shame or guilt begin to shape a conversation and turn into unhelpful judgements and criticisms. Or perhaps your very sense of self is being called into question. Your commitments, competencies, allegiances, values or sense of identity and who you think you are. It might even go so far as to touch on the very roots of our existence and our feelings of being worthy of being loved.

These are some of ways conversations can be hard, as laid out in the book *Difficult Conversations* by Bruce Patton, Douglas Stone and Sheila Heen.

But if conversations can be so difficult, why do we continue to have them? Why should we bother? Isn't it better to avoid them? To run from them until perhaps one day that person is no longer around for us to talk to?

In one way or another, these difficult conversations shape our lives. And often, it is the conversations that we think will be the most difficult that turn out to be the most important. These are the conversations that are worth having.

Introduction to this project

This book came together as a collaboration between Berwick Academy and Berwick Literary Festival. It is a collection of writings from Year 9 students (aged 13 to 14 years) based on the theme of difficult conversations.

As you will see from the variety of entries, the students were invited to think about difficult conversations in lots of different ways. They could explore real conversations that they had had or write about scenarios they imagined. The result is a fascinating collection of poems, short stories, mini-sagas and drama scripts.

The best responses were selected for inclusion in this book. All the entries were anonymised so you will only find the authors listed altogether, a decision made to give the students creative freedom and to not limit the topics they could discuss.

The project was inspired by a piece of local history, a small plaque in Tweedmouth that talks about two meetings and two likely difficult conversations that supposedly happened there in the late 1200s. You can find a history of the plaque and the events it describes within this book.

The book was funded by Create Berwick as part of the Living Heritage programme that aims to celebrate Berwick's local traditions and heritage, and produce an artwork inspired by the town's rich heritage and culture with and for local people.

Finally, it is my hope that as you read this book you will think about the difficult conversations that you've had in your life, and that it will help more people have those conversations that they have been avoiding.

Chris Adriaanse, Editor and curator, August 2024

Introduction from Berwick Literary Festival

When the Festival was founded eleven years ago, it was with the explicit purpose of inviting residents of Berwick and its hinterland, of all ages and backgrounds, into a fresh and creative relationship with the written word and its public performance.

The aim of the festival was both to encourage the emergence of talent for writing from the local population and also to offer audiences the chance to encounter, face-to-face, some of the 'names' in literature and associated arts whose books are familiar, and whose faces are sometimes famous, locally, nationally and even internationally.

At the heart of our Festival programme, in the intervening years, has been the work with all our schools. It has been warmly welcomed at every level and each year we have rejoiced at the positive feedback that we have received from pupils, teachers and parents.

This year, we have expanded further our relationship with Berwick Academy, with the energetic encouragement of Tracy Hush, the Head Teacher until this summer, and Ben Ryder, Assistant Head, by commissioning this project on difficult conversations, with financial support through Create Berwick, and employing Chris Adriaanse, whose reputation as a professional storyteller precedes him, to design and execute the plan.

The project was prompted by a mysterious plaque that appears on the wall of a house in West End, Tweedmouth, pointing us to an equally mysterious event in Berwick's long history of engagement with the endless and often violent story of the English/Scottish Border.

This collection of writings has interwoven a number of the hopes and expectations of the Berwick Literary Festival, including immersing ourselves in the life and heritage of Berwick-upon-Tweed as well as developing a partnership between the Festival and a range of other local organisations and individuals.

Most of all it has been about engaging young people in an exploration of the power of words in our lives, and in so doing, hopefully, enabling us to hear and celebrate the insights and reactions of some of our young people.

Finally, the project has only been achieved with the help of so many different people who live in and love this area – historians, politicians, teachers, students, designers and printers (all acknowledged at the end of this book) – that we can make a substantial and challenging contribution to the written story of our community.

Andrew Deuchar, Festival Director

Introduction from Berwick Academy

We all experience difficult conversations in our day-to-day life; some that we regret, some that we wish that we had had and some that have resulted in a positive outcome. At Berwick Academy, we explicitly teach skills such as dealing with difficult conversations because we know that these 'learning behaviours' will enable our students to flourish, not only as young people, but as adults who will excel in life beyond school.

Our ambition is to provide our students with an educational experience that helps them to develop as young people who are ready for employment and/or further education; have the skills, knowledge and qualifications that enable them to compete at a local, national and international level; and are good citizens able to contribute positively to their local and wider communities. These goals are supported by the core values of the school of Friendship, Learning and Respect and our key principles of 'On Time, On Side and On Task' that are at the heart of our school and provide the foundation from which all else is built.

This project has helped to involve our students with a lesser known but important part of our local history that has significance at a national level. As young people in their early teenage years, our students have engaged well with the theme of difficult conversations, showing a wide variety of topics, styles, approaches and sensitivity to this important topic.

It has also been a delight that we have been able to give our students a unique opportunity to work with members of the local community to create published work that will serve as a lasting reminder of the project and their contributions.

Ben Ryder, Assistant Headteacher, Berwick Academy

A short folktale to begin

This is a story about a servant who could not find the words.

The Drop of Honey

A king was sitting out on his balcony one morning with his advisor. From his seat, the king had a view out across the city, to the hills in the distance, and below to the bustling streets and market squares.

This morning, however, he had barely looked out at the city and was deep in conversation with his advisor as he tucked into one of his favourite breakfasts, fresh bread topped with lashings of honey. So, the king was unaware when, amongst his animated gesturing, a large dollop of honey flew off and landed on the side of the balcony.

One of the servants moved forward to clear up the mess but the advisor, seeing what had happened, discreetly ushered the servant back without the king noticing. While the king was a good man, he was quick to anger so the advisor did not want to draw attention to the mess he had made. *Better to do nothing, to say nothing*, thought the advisor and moved his attention back to his conversation with the king.

Meanwhile the servant kept his eye on the honey. He watched as it warmed gently in the sunshine and a large drop fell from the balcony to the ground below.

The first to notice the drop was a fly, but before it could enjoy this sweet treat, a bird swooped down and ate the fly. As the bird took off, a cat jumped out from the shadows and snatched the bird in its jaws. But before the cat could enjoy its meal, it was set upon by a dog that had freed itself from its leash. The cat and the dog began fighting – biting and scratching, barking and hissing. It was only when the two owners came to the rescue that the animals could be separated and the fighting stopped, but soon they were arguing about who was to blame.

All the while, the servant had been watching from the balcony. *All this from a drop of honey, surely it cannot get any worse,* he thought and continued watching. Below in the market square a small crowd had gathered, each person taking the side of either the cat owner or the dog owner. Tensions were growing. Voices began to be raised. People were being gently pushed and shoved.

Up on the balcony the servant watched the crowd swell further. *All this from a drop of honey,* he thought, *surely it cannot get any worse.* His eyes wandered across the city and to his relief he saw some of the king's guards making their way to the market square. *Phew,* he thought, *finally, this will put an end to things,* and he turned back, turning towards the king and the advisor who were still deep in conversation.

Meanwhile, when the guards arrived things only escalated. People began shouting and pushing. Someone threw a stone. Someone else threw one back. A window broke. Then a fire started.

The fire spread from stall to stall then house to house and a great column of black smoke began rising high above the city. It was only then that the king and the advisor noticed.

They were ushered out of the palace, along with the servant and other key personnel, to a safe distance outside the city walls and far away from the fire.

As the servant sat on the hill, watching the fire spread and the smoke rise, his mind went back to the balcony earlier that morning. He thought about the drop of honey that he had seen fall from the balcony and he wondered, *what if we had done something, said something?*

Retold by Chris Adriaanse

Adapted from a well-known folktale from Southeast Asia

Difficult Conversations

by Berwick Academy students

List of contributors

In alphabetical order:

Abbie Ferguson
Alex Foxton
Alexa Malone
Alfie Dunn
Amy Coyle
Anna Nicoll
Blair Mackay
Bobby Calder
Chad McClymont
Charlotte Flannigan
Ella Malthouse
Harry Flannigan
Heidi Lawrence
Jasmine Bell
Jay Carr
Lana Johnston
Lauren Reid

Layton Galvanauskas
Logan Crooks
Lucy Wickes
Lylah Waterhouse
Madyson Buckland
Maisy Metcalf
Maja Szymczak
Matt Dryden
Miles Dalrymple
Molly Fairbairn
Morgane Guerin
Nathan Nevins
Niamh Brown
Oscar Wilkinson
Scarlett Arnold
Sebastian Lockie
Sophie Cornish

unsaid words

that

embressement*

Then I

[Yell

Unspoken
Words

]

just kept walking

Breaking the Silence

Beneath the weight of unsaid words we stand
A fragile bridge across a silent land
Eyes meet, yet hearts are coated in dense despair
Truth hangs between us, heavy in the air.

Voices quiver, tiptoe through the night.
Seeking solace, searching for the light.
With trembling lips, we breathe the battle still
And face the storm against our weary will.

Borrowing Money

While the guilt floods my brain, I build the courage to ask the question.

"Can I have some money, Dad?"

Throughout my life, I see my dad working away his singular life just to keep me comfortable and happy. I wonder if the new shoes are really necessary? Or the new perfume everyone brags about, that I want?

I remember to be grateful that my dad puts a roof over my head and the extras that come along with that.

Do I need an unnecessary, overpriced, trending object that I beg over and over for? Is it all really worth it?

Me without You

In the quiet room, words hung low —
Facing the truth, we let them flow.
Talking about loss, all that has slipped away,
Trying to find the right words to say.

Each word a weight, a piece of pain.
Letting it go like a gentle rain.
Hopes and dreams fade from view.
Caught in a moment, me without you.

Gone too Soon

G – greeting his wife, holding his uniform and medals
O – openly we begin to cry
N – nothing could make this moment easy
E – every part of me began to tremble

T – the sunsets will be his new creation
O – onwards they will look more beautiful
O – over the horizon he lies

S – silent now but once commander-in-chief
O – once the chief, always the chief
O – once her husband, always the one for her heart
N – never to be forgotten

Moving On

Lips quivering, hands jolting like electrical wires. Doubts hanging in her mind like a garland.

The betrayal was still rich in the atmosphere. Emotions swirled like treacherous storms obliterating any ounces of pity left. Purposefully alienated, mocked, silences. Tears glimmered like prisms as her vision distorted.

Her heart didn't just fall to the floor, it descended through the earth and got scalded at the core. Tidal waves crashed against her head, echoing like a gong, blocking outward noise.

This was the grim, inescapable part of reality – inevitable as it was, her heart still shattered as emotions flooded the desolate room.

Should I stay or should I go?

I wanted to move school,
But I didn't know what to do.
I wanted to tell my mum,
But I didn't know what to say.

I was scared to open up
So I waited a couple days.
And as I lay writing the letter of my fears,
I suddenly felt a tear.

I was so upset to tell her why,
But I did not want her to see me cry.

Isolating myself from school,
Not knowing what to do.

Losing friends and getting left out
Made me think, is it worth it?

Should I stay or should I go?

Secrets Can't be Secrets for Long

There's something bugging me. My stomach drops when I think about the possibility of this being true. I care deeply about her, enough to want to tell her what I've seen witnessed but I can't possibly let the words run freely out my mouth. Too many thoughts are passing through my mind as to what's going to happen if she finds out and then comes to tell. Then I would be filled with guilt and forced to let it out.

So yes, I have to tell her. But how? How am I going to tell her such a thing? Something I can't even think about without feeling a rush of emotions, never mind saying it out loud. I have to build up the courage to admit what I saw. I just need to think of it as building a Lego tower, take it one step at a time and I'll be fine. Won't I?

that day

Rising
Tensions

not | good | enough

only said

Phone Drama

My dad took my phone off of me. He said, "Why are you shouting at your sister again?"

I answered: "Because she is annoying me!"

"Anyway, you always take her side. She's clearly your favourite," I continued.

"Yeah, yeah, whatever," my dad shouted back.

My sister always gets what she wants and all I do is get punished for nothing.

"I'm taking your phone off you for backchat," my dad continued once again.

"What? Why?"

"So you can learn to just be nice," my dad said. "It's these kids' phones, I say".

And the thing is, I didn't do anything.

Cruise Trips

Characters
CAROLINE – mum
JESS – daughter
JAMES – dad

In the living room, Caroline talks to Jess about the cruise trip ...

CAROLINE: We have planned to go on a cruise trip for the summer.

JESS: Mum, I don't want to go and be with lots of people I don't even know. I'd rather just hang out with my friends.

CAROLINE: Jess, you are going on this trip. We have paid a lot of money for this.

Later in the kitchen ...

JAMES: Jess, let's talk about the trip. We want you to go and it will mean a lot to your mum.

JESS: But I don't know why it's so important. I don't want to go. I'm old enough to stay home by myself.

CAROLINE: But this might be our last holiday with you before you move out and you'll have the rest of summer to hang out with your friends.

JESS: You can't change my mind. I'm not going.

CAROLINE: Why are you acting so immature? We are just trying
            to do something nice for you.

JAMES: Please Jess, come on the trip, it will make your mum
            and me happy to get one final holiday with you.

JESS: No! I'm sorry but I've already made plans and I'm not
            changing them.

Jess gets up from the kitchen table and leaves the room ...

What Would You Do?

As a big fat mega monster wearing a bow grasps you in its mighty clutch.

You exclaim and plead that your child is ill and that you're financially struggling.

The gigantic beast gargles and roars as it's overwhelmed by this story. She doesn't look convinced.

In your peripheral version, you see your friend and wager that instead of your flesh, the monster eats your friend.

A shocked face wipes across the monster and a slim slit spreads across its face and a slippery tongue licks its lips.

Quickly, you're dropped and the monster swipes and consumes what was your best friend.

An Argumentative Turn

After Insy and I finally got out of the water spout and got to his house, his parents were standing cross-armed. So when he got inside, a massive argument arose.

We were trying to say it wasn't our fault, that it had rained and I couldn't get up the rainy road.

But our parents counterpoint (which was very valid) was that we could have just kept walking along the wall next to the road instead of trying to go the fun way.

We then replied that all our friends were watching us so we had to.

"Go to your room!"

Tour Tensions: The Swiftie Uproar

Taylor Swift fans were furious after Dave Grohl made a controversial comment during an interview.

"We call our tour the 'Errors Tour' because we play live," he remarked, seemingly suggesting that Taylor Swift doesn't.

The Swifties couldn't believe it. Social media exploded with angry posts and hashtags like #apologiseDave.

Some Swifties even went to the extent of saying Dave was a greasy old man who only said it to gain more attention as his band 'Foo Fighters' were losing popularity.

While some pushed it as far as saying: "I had to google who Dave Grohl was. He looks awful."

Cherished Memories

A building overhears that it will be demolished ...

"Unfortunately, we are going to have to demolish this building. We need to build a road to take people to the new shopping centre outside the town." That is what the *Morning Post* said today.

Why would they want to demolish me? I'm the place that brings the most tourists to the town. I can't close. I don't want to close. What will the kids do when they want an ice cream after going to the beach? What about the adults who come here for something a bit stronger after a hard day at work? My pub quizzes and karaoke nights are what keeps people coming to this old town. I add the fun to this place. Nobody but old people who want to retire would come to this place if I wasn't here.

What will happen when I am no longer here?

I guess this will be a retirement village with no young people. We will no longer need the schools or the souvenir shops. They will be replaced with sheltered accommodation. We will no longer need play parks but instead flower parks, which elderly people could walk around in their Zimmer frames.

I will always remember the children running into the shop, wrapped up in towels with their parents hurrying behind them.

The perfect beach day! Then, at night, the party lights would shimmer above the bar and adults would come for a drink and a laugh with old friends.

Finally, once the party was over, the owners would ascend the old staircase with a smile on their faces. What wonderful memories I have and I know they will be shared by the many families who enjoyed their stay here even after I'm gone. So many memories that will all be demolished with me and for what? A road! At least the road will take people to a new place to make new memories.

However, there will be no more families stopping as they will be driving through the town instead of staying. The only people who will be staying now will be the elderly and the few young people who want a quiet place to start their lives.

Unfortunately, my neighbours will also be demolished. As well as this, their owners can't afford to lose their business. Unlike mine who were going to retire soon anyways, they will have to find somewhere new to start all over again. They all have 2 weeks to be packed up and out. I don't know where my owners are going to go, and they have no relatives nearby to stay with. All I can think about is the difficult conversations they are going to have tonight.

The Broken Phone

My mum came home from work. She was in a good mood. She was asking how my day was. I thought she wouldn't have yelled once I told her.

I was wrong. I told her and her face went red, and she was full of anger.

She yelled at me for hours until she finally found an old hardly working Samsung phone, which was probably as useful as a dull knife, but I took it without a word waiting for her to get back into her original good mood.

She never did become happy that day. That's my lesson taught.

in the park

couldn't believe it

Caught
in the Act

crying

Doing The Dishes

When my mother walked through the door into the kitchen, she saw an overloaded sink full of dishes. Meanwhile I was playing on my gaming console.

My mother asked why the dishes weren't clean or dry. I was about to reply when she said I was grounded until I had done my chores. I froze for a second and didn't know what to say. So I yelled: "For what!"

She sighed and said, "Don't yell at me young man!"

I said I would never do chores ever again.

Then after the event, I waited in my room in pure boredom for 10 minutes, but it felt like an hour without any social devices.

The silence got to me, so I walked to the sitting room sobbing and I apologised for shouting. She said I would be ungrounded if I do the rest of my chores.

I was allowed my social devices after doing my chores.

Walking the Dog

Before my mam went away, she asked me to walk the dog. About 30 to 40 mins after she left, I texted her saying I've taken the dog on a walk. When she got back, she asked my sister if I went for a walk and she said "No".

I could hear them speaking as my mam was coming up the stairs. I was thinking of an excuse of why I didn't go. Then she asked me why I didn't take the dog for a walk. I said, "I couldn't be bothered", and that's when the conversation got into an argument.

Bike Crash

I scratched my bike.
It was bad, very bad.
My dad heard that I crashed.
He asked if I scratched it.
I had told him no.
I knew it was wrong,
Not like me at all,
But I didn't want to tell him at all.
I didn't want to look spoiled.

Good news, good news,
Got a new bike.
Bad news, bad news,
Scratched that one too.

The Assembly Incident

In the school hall,
Where the teachers stand tall,
They asked about an incident that occurred in the fall,
This included a boy, a bike and a ball!

The boy was riding along in the park
When Billy and Bob kicked the ball like a spark,
Striking the boy called Christopher Clark
His whole vision went blurry and very, very dark.

Now in the hall, Billy and Bob felt rather small
So as the teachers stared,
They felt very scared!

Sat in fear, they knew their awkward conversation
with the headteacher was near,
So they come up with a plan, a great idea,
to blame it on a boy who was in their year.

Now as they decided to give it a try,
A teacher overheard their ridiculous lie,
This ultimately led to Billy and Bob being expelled
from Stanford High.

The Test Tension

In class one day, when tension grew Tobias whispered to Emily "Psst hey you!" He begged for her to be quick and cheat.

Emily flustered, "No way Tobias," she said. He tried his luck but yet he was still stuck.

The teacher caught his eyes then Tobias knew he had nowhere to hide. The teacher said "Come to the front Tobias and you can explain why you were cheating off of Emily's test."

Red faced and stammering, Tobias stood trembling regretfully. "I ... I ... I was stuck and I cheated off of Emily's test," he stuttered out.

The class in silence and eyes on him. Tobias a horrible sight. He knew that there was no light. A lesson learned filled with embarrassment.

The Phone call

Facing
the Truth

Is it really worth it?

difficult convers

I told her .

↑

•

@

←

[▨]

Failed Exams

As the boy looked at his grades, he knew he was going to have to tell his parents the bad news and he knew they weren't going to be happy.

When he got home, his parents looked expectantly at him.

"Well," said his mum, "what did you get?"

"I need to sit down," said the boy, as he thought about how to say this.

"I kind of failed," he said quietly.

"You what?!!" shouted back his mum. "I thought you said you were confident."

"I was. I don't know what happened," said the boy.

"I'm sorry", he added quietly.

Crash!

"Mum don't get mad," I pleaded. "You've got to promise."

She already knew something was wrong. She motioned to continue so I did.

I explained I'd broken the window playing football inside and was incredibly sorry.

She stared daggers at me.

Tensions rising, she stood and walked towards the shattered glass.

Disappointment shone brightly on her face, cancelling out the anger.

Why did she do that? Now I felt even worse. My heart dropped hearing her voice. I grabbed a dustpan and brush and cleaned up the mess.

Her disappointment made me feel so uncomfortable, I wished for anger.

She Will Fight

We all gathered in the living room, awaiting the news our parents had to tell my brothers and me.

The tension tightened and the silence grew louder until our dad broke it.

He began saying how we were not to worry, and that it will be okay. He continued, mentioning the topic of the conversation, our granny's health.

It turned out that it wasn't good, she had cancer. The shock spread across the room like a bullet. It also turned out that it wasn't fully curable. Our world felt like it was caving in.

But we know she will fight ...

Crushed Dreams

As Tim arrives to the camp, like he does every morning, the pitches are silent – no training, no people.

Tim enters the building ready to play, but he is pulled aside. "I'd like to see you in my office," Coach says. Tim follows.

When he arrives, his manager tells him take a seat.

Not long after, the coach says: "No other way to say this, but you're not good enough for us. You need to leave. Your contract will be terminated."

All Tim can do is agree.

As he leaves, tears pour down his face. He will have to perform better.

The Same Excuse

When my mum was asking me questions, she kept asking the same question. I told her and she said "Sorry, it's my ADHD". Then I said, "You use that as an excuse for everything" and she shouted at me, so I stormed up to my room.

Ten minutes later I went down to say sorry. Then we made up.

Failed Audition

After what I thought was the best audition of my life, my dance teacher said to me: "You danced amazingly, but unfortunately not good enough to make the team this year."

My heart felt like it was ripping out of my chest. As he continued to speak, I couldn't hear a word he said. It was like everything around me was spinning. I have never felt this pain.

I have always made the team. Why was now any different?

My dance teacher was reassuring me, saying: "Practice makes perfect!"

But everything he said was just making me even more melancholic.

Not the One

Paul went through a breakup recently and was sad about it. So he went on a date. He didn't like the date, but she really liked him and thought it's going really well.

Paul thought otherwise. He didn't like the date's energy and personality.

When they were both home from the date, she messaged him: "Want to go on another date?"

Now Paul has to deal with this difficult conversation.

But Paul says "Hey, I really enjoyed the date, but I don't think you're the one for me. I am really sorry."

The Phone Call

ME: Dad ... I've had a crash.

DAD: How bad?

ME: Quite bad.

DAD: What happened?

ME: I was going too fast over a jump and went over the handlebars.

DAD: Are you okay? Is your bike okay?

ME: I'm fine, my bike isn't.

DAD: What have you broken?

ME: Forks, bars and stem.

DAD: Seriously? How much is it going to cost?

ME: Over £200 ...

DAD: WHAT! We will have to discuss it when you are home.

ME: Okay Dad, I'm sorry.

DAD: It's fine son, these things happen.

Fallout

Friendships can be like a delicate glass, easily shattered. A simple misunderstanding led to a fallout, creating a chasm between us.

As the days passed, the silence grew heavier, burdening us both. Finally, we decided to confront the elephant in the room.

The difficult conversation was filled with raw emotions, unspoken words and pent-up frustration.

Yet, as we shared our perspectives and listened with open hearts, a glimmer of understanding emerged.

Slowly, the rift began to heal, and our friendship emerged stronger from the depths of that challenging conversation.

They Don't All Have Spots and Four Legs

What do I say to him? He doesn't know that I know I love him though and he loved me ... or at least I thought he did. Should I confront him? Oh, how difficult this conversation is to be ...

"Erm, I don't really know how to else to really confront you but ... I know what you have done."

"Look, I'm sorry. I didn't mean to. I didn't know what to do."

"What do you mean you didn't know what to do? I was at home in our house! And I'm not accepting your apology after that."

"I promise my love, it will never happen ever again."

Once a cheat always a cheat as the saying goes. Now he's got me thinking, was he really worth the last six years of my life? No, no he wasn't ...

"What I'm trying to say to you is that we are done. We are finished."

"No, please darling, don't let this ruin us."

"What else do you expect you have been cheating on me for the last four and a half months."

"Oh, you know everything, don't you."

"Yes, I do. Now I suggest you start packing and find somewhere else to move into."

Wow, that felt good to get off my chest! Boys are of no use these days, once a cheat, always a cheat. I'm off to celebrate my new single life and find myself a man. I hope he finds somewhere else to live!

MJ

On 25th June 2009, news broke about a famous person's death. My mum opened my door with a look like someone close had something happen.

She then said the words being spoken worldwide, "Michael Jackson has passed away."

My brain started rushing. *How did he die? Why? When? How?*

My mum then explained what happened. He died and it affected the world.

Striving

One dark and stormy night, when I was at my house, my mum told me about my ever-growing number of negative points on my club charts.

She said that she was not happy that I had accumulated this crazed total amount of negative points.

I myself was also unimpressed with myself and I felt very disappointed that I had driven my mum to the point of telling me how angry she was with me.

Ever since that day, I have never gotten a detention and I have only had one negative for handing my maths homework in late.

Finding Support

I'm Sorry

Apprehensively, I step into the kitchen.

"Mum …" she stares at me, "I'm sorry."

"There's no need darling," she mumbles, "You just need help."

"I know … I …" I can't form sentences, I break down. Mum comes and wraps her arms around my sore body.

"I'll get you help, I promise darling."

We stay like this for a while. I feel ashamed.

She rubs my arms. She shouldn't be treating me this way. She should be angry, horrified, disgusted!

She is keeping me close. She is keeping me safe …

A Challenge We Now Face Together

Things happen that we might not appreciate, but it's better to talk about it than ignore it. People can break up, leave or get ill.

I knew about my dad's recent hospital trips already, but I don't think anything could've prepared me for this conversation.

My parents had called everyone downstairs and, as we sat down, the atmosphere instantly turned dark.

He had cancer.

My sister cried and I was lost for words. Questions were playing in our heads like a song on repeat for ages.

No one likes having difficult conversations, but they're as challenging as they are helpful.

Confessions

Ellie's mum was called by the school. Now she has to confess everything.

All of these questions rushed through her mind: "How do I explain this? What will she say? Is she going to hate me now?"

Ellie is petrified to talk to mum about anything.

Fortunately, she went and had that conversation and received nothing but love and support.

It does get better!

It'll Get Better

Sometimes I find conversations hard. For example, talking about my family, especially my dad.

There has been a lot of things that have happened in the past that make me uncomfortable or I find difficult to talk about.

Young people like me need to realise that people are there to talk to and the more we talk the less difficult it gets.

I hope this makes at least one person feel better knowing that someone else struggles with the same thing as them.

My sensitive topic can be all different kinds of things, but my dad in particular.

Everything will get better!

I Need a Break

Colton, a middle-aged man in a suit sits across from Calista,
a young woman in a casual dress. They are both tense.

COLTON: *(Clearing his throat)* **"Calista can I talk to you for a moment?"**

CALISTA: *(Nervously)* **"Sure, Colton."**

COLTON: *(Hesitates)* **I've noticed that there have been some issues with your work performance lately.**

CALISTA: *(Surprised)* **Oh, I didn't know. I'm ever so sorry.**

COLTON: *(Harshly)* **Your deadline submissions have been late and the quality of your work has declined.**

CALISTA: *(Stammering)* **I've been going through a lot lately. Mymother is sick, and I've been spending most of my day caring for her – –**

COLTON: *(Interrupting)* **I understand that you're dealing with a difficult situation, but your performance is unacceptable.**

CALISTA: *(Frustrated)* **It's not that simple! I can't just drop everything and focus on work when my mother is sick and struggling.**

COLTON: *(Firmly)* **I'm not asking you to ignore your**

responsibilities, but you need to find a way to manage both.

CALISTA: *(Tears welling up in her eyes)* I'm trying my best Colton, I'm not trying to be lazy.

COLTON: *(Slightly softening)* I know you're not, Calista. But we need to come up with a solution that works for both of us.

CALISTA: *(Hesitantly)* What do you suggest?

COLTON: *(Pausing)* ... I propose that you take a temporary leave of absence. You can use this time to focus on your personal responsibilities without the stress of work.

CALISTA: *(Torn)* But I don't want to let you down.

COLTON: *(Gently)* You won't. We will figure this out together.

END

A final folktale to end

This is the story of a woman unable to confront the monster in her garden.

The Beast of the Bean Garden

Augusta Cump had always had green fingers. Even as a child it seemed whatever she planted would grow and flourish. While growing up she had experimented and grown many different things, her favourite thing to grow were broad beans. Fresh from the stalks, she would crack open the hard pods and serve the boiled beans with plenty of butter – there was nothing tastier.

As an adult, she worked hard, saved up and bought a house in the countryside with a large garden. She turned the whole piece of land into a bean garden, working hard to harvest her precious beans during the summer months.

Whenever she had any beans left, she would give them away to her friends and neighbours, so soon the reputation of her beans – which were indeed the freshest and tastiest in the land – spread far and wide. People would come for miles for a handful of fresh beans, whatever Augusta could spare.

However, soon demand outstripped supply. People began arriving in large numbers and would queue outside her door each day over the summer, waiting for whatever beans they could get. Sometimes fights would break out and Augusta would look on in dismay.

Augusta also noticed that her beans were going missing from her garden. She saw footprints in the soil that didn't belong to her. It was frightening and happened night after night so in the end she had no choice.

Over the winter, she had the walls of her garden doubled in height and she laid vicious traps and snares to catch whichever fool might dare wander into her garden. The precautions worked and the next summer none of her beans went missing and she was able to provide enough extra ones to keep her visitors happy.

But towards the end of the growing season, she heard a terrible crash and cry coming from the bean garden late one night. Peeking out from behind the curtain, she could make out a shadowy figure of the window that looked strange and twisted in the soft moonlight.

The next morning, nothing could have prepared her for when she saw the creature in the daylight. It was hideous. It had three heads with each mouth filled with hundreds of teeth. It stood at least seven foot high and was covered in scales. The creature also had great claws at the end of its arms that looked like they could rip anyone to shreds.

At first Augusta didn't know what to do. She stayed out of her garden and away from the creature, hoping that if she just ignored it then it would go away. Two weeks passed and the monster was still in the garden. What's more, he had begun eating the very last of the season's broad beans.

Finally, when there were only a few more bean pods remaining on the vines, she made a plan. She would go out and confront the beast. She picked up her largest and most ferocious looking broom, wielding it like her sword, and puffing up her chest and shoulders, she went outside.

As she snuck up to the beast from behind and got closer to it, she noticed for the first time that the creature hadn't been eating the beans, only the bean pods. To its side, neatly piled were stacks of deshelled broad beans. Augusta was delighted. She swept in and picked up the beans, relieved that she no longer needed to face the beast.

So that's how a strange alliance was born. For the next fifty years, the beast lived in the garden. The two never spoke a word to each other nor acknowledged each other's existence. The beast would eat the tough bean pods and Augusta would gather up the beans that it left behind. No one else would dare enter the garden so her beans were also safe from thieves.

Augusta was now an old woman and it made getting around the garden harder and more tiring. Early one spring, she was laying some new hazel poles to support the emerging shoots, but no matter how hard she tried, she couldn't manage to tie them together.

Finally in exasperation, she cried out: "Beast, see these sticks," pointing in large gestures and speaking slowly and loudly. "Hold them, like this," she finished, gesturing with her hands and nodding her head.

The creature turned all three of its heads towards her, looking at her for the first time, raised its claws and started speaking.

"Dear Miss Cump, I would be delighted to assist you, however, my foot is trapped in one of your snares. These claws of mine are so clumsy that I've not been able to free myself. I've had nothing to eat except those dreadful bean pods – much tastier at least then what's inside of them."

Augusta's mouth opened wide, shocked not only that the beast could talk but that he disliked her precious beans.

"Dear me," said Augusta. "I had no idea. If only you had said something all those years ago. I thought you were happy staying here and had chosen to make it your home."

"I was waiting for you to say something," the beast said. "I was so embarrassed at having been caught, I didn't want to say anything. Then the more time that passed, the harder it got to say anything at all."

Augusta bent down and carefully released the beast from the snare.

"I suppose you'll be leaving now," said Augusta, tears rolling down her cheeks as she realised how much she would miss the beast and how much its company over the last five decades had meant to her.

"Do you take me for some kind of monster?" said the beast. "That would be most discourteous after all we've been through together. Please call me Brulder. I'd be delighted to stay if you'll have me. But could I ask for two things?"

"Anything at all, Brulder," said Augusta, still wiping the tears from her face.

"Would you mind bringing me some straw for a bed? And I should like you to grow me some cauliflower as they are my favourite things to eat," said Brulder.

So Augusta hurried off the get some straw and find cauliflower seeds to sow.

In the years that followed, Brulder provided support and companionship to Augusta for the last few years of her life. As for the cauliflowers she grew, they turned out to be the best cauliflowers that anyone had ever grown but no one got any except for Brulder.

As for Augusta, she always wondered what life might have been like if only she had had the courage to speak to Brulder all those years ago. It turned out that, despite her initial fears, he was not as bad as he looked.

Retold by Chris Adriaanse

Adapted with permission from Dreadful Stories Volume II: Another treasury of awful folk tales from the British Isles and a bit of a Norse myth by Kitty Brownbelt

A mysterious plaque
in Tweedmouth

This project was inspired by the following piece of local history, about two seemingly difficult conversations that are said to have taken place near the banks of the river Tweed.

The plaque in Parliament Square

If you cross the old bridge in Berwick-Upon-Tweed towards Tweedmouth, walk under the new bridge and head towards the houses, you'll find yourself on a small green surrounded by buildings. On the front of the house opposite the pub, you will see an ageing metal plaque mounted on a wooden frame. It is small and sits just above eye level, such that you might pass it a hundred times and never notice it. The plaque reads:

> In 1278 under Edward I of England and Alexander III of Scotland, a 'Parliament of magnates' from both countries assembled here to settle the boundary line between England and Scotland. This was necessary because of a great dispute on that point, which had arisen between the King of Scots and Robert de Insula, Bishop of the County Palatine of Durham.
>
> In 1296 Edward I called another Parliament here to receive the fealty of certain Scottish ranks.

If you are like me, then two questions might pop into your head as you read the text: who put the plaque there? And what actually happened at these meetings?

As we'll see, the answers get a little complicated as both questions get shrouded by the passage of time.

The site of the plaque

This corner of the West End of Tweedmouth, where the plaque can be found, is known locally as "Parliament Square". No record of the name survives on historical maps apart from the Ordnance Survey map of 1852 that shows a "Parliament Close".

In days gone by the route along the river through the West End seems likely to have been the main road to Norham Castle, Kelso and beyond, but the area was transformed most recently in the 20th century with the building of The Royal Tweed Bridge. Nowadays, you're unlikely to find yourself passing through the West End unless you intended it.

The Royal Tweed Bridge was built between 1925 and 1928, totally changing the shape of the area. Having been built in the mid-war period, much of the north end of the village centre was decimated indiscriminately to make way for the bridge. The area around the current plaque was used as a working yard during the bridge's construction and was subsequently used as a lorry park.

The square was selected by Berwick Borough Council in the early 1970s for redevelopment. The project was designed by Reavell and Cahill, a family firm of architects in Alnwick that worked from 1886 to 2005. They reestablished two street facades adjacent to the village green and built a third to form a triangle, screening off the new bridge. Twenty-nine houses were built, some restored or modernised, but most were entirely new.

The housing development was completed in 1975 and won two awards. One was a Civic Trust House and Cottage Award and the other was a coveted Conservation Award from the

Royal Institute of Chartered Surveyors, awarded in 1976, which recognised the "great sensitivity" of the project and its social and environmental improvement.

As for the plaque, which was mounted on one of the houses, it is not clear who instigated, designed or installed it. There are no details on the plaque itself. There is limited information in the Berwick and Northumberland archives. The architects have closed and the partners are no longer with us, so who decided to put it there and why is now lost to history.

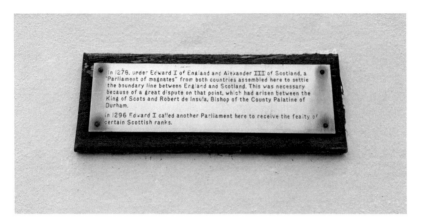

The events of the plaque

As for the events the plaque describes, first we need a little more context. In the 1200s, England and Scotland were separate countries, with the border much as it is today, apart from the notable exception of Berwick. The Treaty of York, signed in 1236, divided the Anglo-Scottish border into western, middle and eastern "marches" on both sides, providing a buffer zone to help manage the violence and cross-border raids in the area. The Treaty ushered in a more peaceful period between England and Scotland, during which the Tweed valley became an economic heartland for Scotland.

Berwick-upon-Tweed at that time was three separate communities divided across two countries. Berwick was the most prosperous town in Scotland and a major port. Wool was the main product and merchants from Europe set up homes and businesses there, generating massive revenues. Tweedmouth was a small village in England lacking fortifications – the building of a castle had been attempted in the early 1200s, but was destroyed and the workers killed under orders of the King of Scotland. Spittal lay on the main road from Holy Island to Berwick and was probably not much more than the religious hospital from which it is named.

At the time, Tweedmouth and the surrounding area were controlled by the Bishop of Durham, in addition to Bedlington (Bedlingtonshire), Holy Island (Islandshire) and, of course, the county of Durham.

The first meeting – a difficult conversation?

The plaque talks of a "parliament of magnates" and a "great dispute" occurring at the site of the plaque:

> In 1278 under Edward I of England and Alexander III of Scotland, a 'Parliament of magnates' from both countries assembled here to settle the boundary line between England and Scotland. This was necessary because of a great dispute on that point, which had arisen between the King of Scots and Robert de Insula, Bishop of the County Palatine of Durham.

However, the history books begin to tell a slightly different story. According to the published itinerary of his movements, King Edward I of England was certainly not present. As for the notion of a "parliament", John Scott's *Berwick-Upon-Tweed:*

The History of the Town and Guild, published in 1888, instead speaks of a "great meeting of magnates of both countries at Tweedmouth".

The earlier John of Fordun's *Chronicle of the Scottish Nation*, published in 1872, tells us who might have been there: "... three bishops of Scotland ... with a great many earls and other nobles ... while, on behalf of the king of England ... the bishops of Norwich and Durham, the Sheriff of Newcastle, and a great many other knights and clergy".

However, it is not clear from the account if the two sides actually met. Fordun states the Scottish nobles met "at Berwick-on-Tweed" and the English nobles met "at Tweedmouth", but not if the two groups actually congregated nor where that might have been. The affair also took place in Lent, which was taken very seriously in those days with intense fasting and penance, suggesting a more sombre and subdue occasion.

There is record of a letter to King Edward I of England from King Alexander III of Scotland concerning a complaint by the Bishop of Durham in 1277, a year earlier, who had complained about Scottish encroachments on the marches, along the south bank of the Tweed. It was also discussed at parliament, according to the *Oxford Dictionary of National Biography*.

However, despite there being "much correspondence between" the two kings on the topic, Joseph Bain's *Calendar of Documents Relating to Scotland* suggests that this 'great dispute' might have been about "nothing more than a salmon fishery" rather than settling the boundary line as mentioned in the plaque. So while there is certainly truth amidst the claims, what actually took place on the banks of the Tweed is also lost to history.

The time between the two meetings

In the period between the first supposed meeting in 1278 and the second meeting in 1296, the fragile peace between England and Scotland collapsed, leading to over 300 years of near constant war. It started with the death of King Alexander III of Scotland.

In March 1286, the king had been travelling on a stormy night, become separated from his advisors and was found dead the next day. He had no surviving children and so six Guardians were elected at a Scottish Parliament to decide on the successor and proclaimed that Alexander's granddaughter Margaret, the Maid of Norway, would be Queen. However, she was only 3 years old at the time and lived in Norway.

King Edward I of England, who had now successfully conquered much of Wales, was interested in becoming more involved in Scotland's affairs and proposed that Margaret marry his son Edward. However, before the marriage could be officiated, Margaret died while travelling to Scotland in 1290. This plunged Scotland into a second succession crisis that looked like it might erupt into violence.

The Scottish Guardians sought the help of King Edward I of England in 1291 to select the next King of Scotland. He arrived at the Scottish border in April 1291 and thirteen months later, on 30 November 1292, King Edward decided that John Balliol had the strongest claim to the throne and would become King of Scotland.

However, tensions escalated further after King Edward demanded the new Scottish king pay homage to him, effectively establishing Edward as overlord. Then in 1295 while France and England were at war, after refusing to provide troops, Scotland signed a treaty with France to assist each other if either country were attached.

In early 1296, King Edward marched north to the Scottish border, assembling a huge army of more than 25,000 foot soldiers and 4,000 cavalry. On 12 March 1296, King Edward famously crossed the border, attacking and capturing Berwick, and beginning an almost constant state of war between England and Scotland that lasted for more than 300 years.

The second meeting –
another difficult conversation?

There is no doubt that 1296 was a pivotal and devastating year for the people who lived on the banks of the Tweed and beyond. Allegiances were forged and broken, borders were transgressed and rewritten, and the casualties and destruction were devastating. But let us return to the text from the plaque:

> In 1296 Edward I called another Parliament here to receive the fealty of certain Scottish ranks.

During the early years of the war and in the years leading to it, there were many notable signings of fealty to King Edward I of England. The most famous happened over the river, after the conquest of Berwick, where the Scottish nobility were forced to recognise King Edward I of England as their lord in Berwick Castle on 28 August 1296.

In return for restoration of their estates, the Scottish nobles had to submit to the authority of King Edward. If they refused, the consequence was summary execution – death without full and fair trial – so not so much a difficult conversation but more an unequivocal ultimatum.

As for a parliament in Tweedmouth – as the plaque claims – where Scottish nobles swore fealty, there is scant evidence in the history books. There is no mention of a parliament in Tweedmouth nor mention of swearing fealty there.

King Edward I of England did spend much of his time in the borders a few years earlier, between 1291 and 1292, staying in either Norham Castle or Berwick Castle. Journeying between the two, he likely passed through or close to the current site of the plaque quite frequently. The history books do also tell of other signings of fealty in those years, however, nothing on record suggests that any of this happened in Tweedmouth, so it seems the plaque is mistaken.

Berwick-upon-Tweed Castle; engraving by William Miller after Turner, 1833

One final difficult conversation

So was there ever really a parliament in Tweedmouth? Certainly, there is some truth to the first meeting, although what exactly happened, we shall never know, but a scaled down version of what the plaque claims seems possible, but no parliament. There is no evidence for the events of the second meeting, although certainly many Scottish nobles swore fealty to King Edward I of England, but not at a parliament in Tweedmouth.

John Scott's *Berwick-Upon-Tweed: The History of the Town and Guild* suggests that it was a different Edward that led to the naming of "Parliament Square". Scott states that during the siege of Berwick nearly 50 years later in 1333, King Edward III of England "pitched his tent in Tweedmouth, on which he has left an enduring mark; for we have Parliament Street in Tweedmouth to this day." However, both Parliament Street and Parliament Close have since disappeared.

So the difficult conversation seems to be less about whatever the nobles might have been disagreeing about, but rather that the mysterious plaque in Tweedmouth might better be described as a local legend than as local history.

What is for certain though is that Berwick-Upon-Tweed has a fascinating history and, who knows, perhaps there are a few more clues out there waiting to be found.

About the editor

Chris Adriaanse is a storyteller, writer and spoken word artist based in Berwick-upon-Tweed. He was born in London and grew up in rural Oxfordshire, moving to Berwick in 2022.

He studied chemistry and Japanese at the University of Sheffield and then completed a PhD in computational chemistry at the University of Cambridge. After graduating, he became a professional writer, first writing chemistry news and then as a freelance medical writer in the pharmaceutical sciences.

While exploring his creative side, he discovered oral story-telling in 2017. He completed an intensive 3-month training at the International School of Storytelling in East Sussex, followed by a 3-year training with Shonaleigh Cumbers, a Jewish tradition bearer from an unbroken oral tradition.

Chris tells an ever-growing selection of eclectic folktales, wonder tales, myths and legends, and he has a fondness for the weird, the wonderful and the magical. He has told at storytelling clubs, in schools, universities and libraries, and at museums and festivals across the UK.

He sees stories as spaces where difficult questions can be asked. He enjoys exploring complex themes from a place of genuine curiosity. He has a love for language and a fascination with the ways in which the precise use of words can bring images to life.

Acknowledgements

I would like to thank all those who helped and supported this project. It would not have been possible without generous funding by Create Berwick, Northumberland County Council and North East Combined Authority. I am also indebted to Federico García Arias who helped shape this project during its inception.

From Berwick Literary Festival, I would like to thank Andrew Deuchar, Joyce Miller and Jennifer Heald for their invaluable support and assistance.

From Berwick Academy, I would like to thank Tracy Hush, Ben Ryder, Soenem Wahid, Nicola Allenby as well as all the other teachers who were involved in delivering lessons on the history of the plaque, exploring the topic of difficult conversations and generating submissions for book. I would also like to thank all the students in Year 9 without whom this book would have not been possible.

For insights into the plaque, I would like to thank Georgina Hill, Andrew Ayre, Allan Swan, Hermione Hoffmann, Thomas Stewart, Janet Chapman and the staff at Northumberland Archives, Woodhorn.

For discussions into the history, I would like to thank Linda Bankier, Lindsay Allason-Jones, Jim Herbert, Derek Sharman, John Sadler, Michael Prestwich and the staff at the Berwick Record Office.

For producing the book, I would like to thank Anna Parker at Fogbank Projects for the design and Martins The Printers for the printing.

Lastly, I would like to thank Danny Turner for his generous time and support from the very beginning of this project until the very end.

While every effort has been made to ensure the accuracy of this work, all remaining errors are my own.

Finally, I would like to thank you, dear reader, for opening your heart to these difficult conversations. May you go and have some of those worthwhile conversations you have been avoiding. Tread carefully.

chris@chrisadriaanse.co.uk